Clarion Books
a Houghton Mifflin Company imprint
215 Park Avenue South, New York, NY 10003

Published in the United States in 2001 by arrangement with
The Albion Press Ltd, Spring Hill, Idbury, Oxfordshire OX7 6RU, England

www.houghtonmifflinbooks.com

Library of Congress Cataloging-in-Publication Data
Philip, Neil
   Noah and the devil : a legend of Noah's Ark from Romania / retold by Neil
Philip ; illustrated by Isabelle Brent.
       p.   cm.
   Summary: A retelling of the story of Noah's ark, embellished with
elements from Romanian folklore, including how the devil sneaked aboard, the
reason Noah threw a cat overboard, and the role of a snake in saving the ark.
   ISBN 0-618-11754-7
   1. Noah (Biblical figure)—Folklore. [1. Noah (Biblical figure)—Folklore.
2. Noah's ark—Folklore. 3. Folklore– –Romania.] I. Brent, Isabelle, ill. II. Title.
PZ8.1.P55 Gr 2002
398.2'09498'02—dc21
[E]   00-060325

Printed in Hong Kong/China by South China Printing Co.

10 9 8 7 6 5 4 3 2 1

FOR DINAH STEVENSON

N.P.

FOR ELIZABETH LEWIS

I.B.

NOAH AND THE DEVIL

A LEGEND OF NOAH'S ARK FROM ROMANIA

Retold by Neil Philip

Illustrated by Isabelle Brent

CLARION BOOKS

New York

You have probably heard about Noah and the great flood. But not many people know that among the animals on Noah's ark was the Devil himself, in the shape of a mouse.

This is how it happened.

Noah was a big man, and a good man, and he had three sons, and their names were Shem, and Ham, and Japheth.

And God spoke to Noah, saying, "I am sorry now that I ever created human beings. They are lazy and wicked and always fighting. Therefore, I am going to flood the earth, and drown them all."

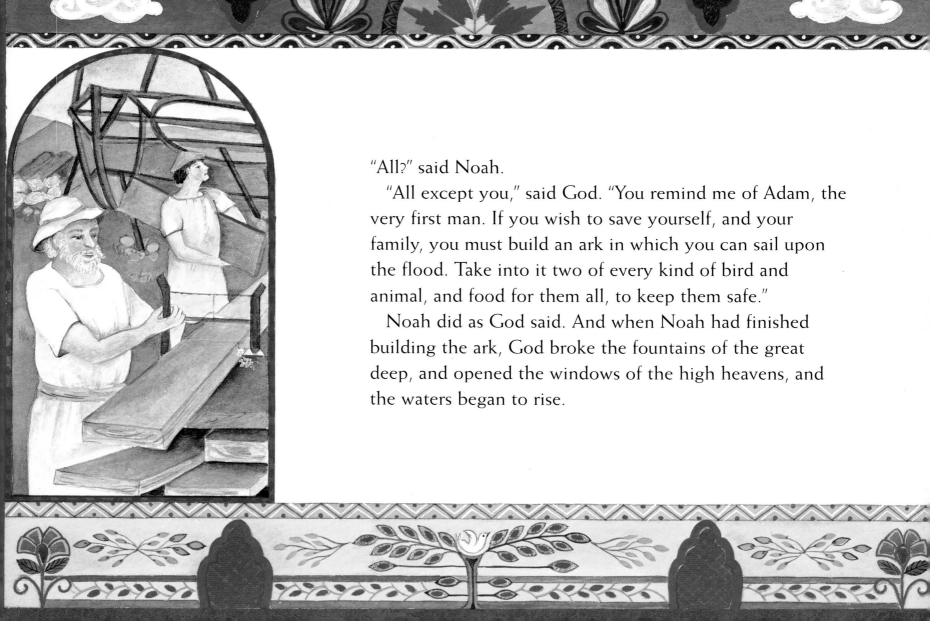

"All?" said Noah.

"All except you," said God. "You remind me of Adam, the very first man. If you wish to save yourself, and your family, you must build an ark in which you can sail upon the flood. Take into it two of every kind of bird and animal, and food for them all, to keep them safe."

Noah did as God said. And when Noah had finished building the ark, God broke the fountains of the great deep, and opened the windows of the high heavens, and the waters began to rise.

Noah held the door of the ark open wide, and his sons, Shem, and Ham, and Japheth, led the animals inside, two by two. And then Shem, and Ham, and Japheth and their wives went on board. And at last there was only Noah's wife left standing up to her knees in water.

"Come in," said Noah. But Noah's wife did not want to go a-sailing on strange seas. She wanted to stay at home. So when Noah said, "Come in," she said, "No."

"Come in," begged Noah. But although the water was now up to her thighs, still she answered, "No." She really was a stubborn woman.

Now the water was up to her waist, and Noah began to get angry. "Oh, you devil, come in!" he said.

And that was just what the Devil wanted to hear. He had been lurking outside, waiting for an invitation to come on board. So when Noah's wife stepped onto the ark, so did the Devil, in the form of a little mouse.

For forty days and forty nights God let the seas rise and the rain fall, until the whole earth was once again covered in water, as it had been at the beginning of time. Even the highest mountaintops were lost beneath the waves, and all the creatures that lived on the earth were drowned.

The only ones to be saved were the animals and birds on Noah's ark, and Noah and his wife, and Shem, and Ham, and Japheth and their wives. They all lived together in the wooden ship that Noah had built, and whenever they began to quarrel—if the lion began to roar, or the dog to bark, or if Shem, or Ham, or Japheth spoke sharply to his wife—Noah would tap them on the nose and say, "No fighting!" And so the peace was kept.

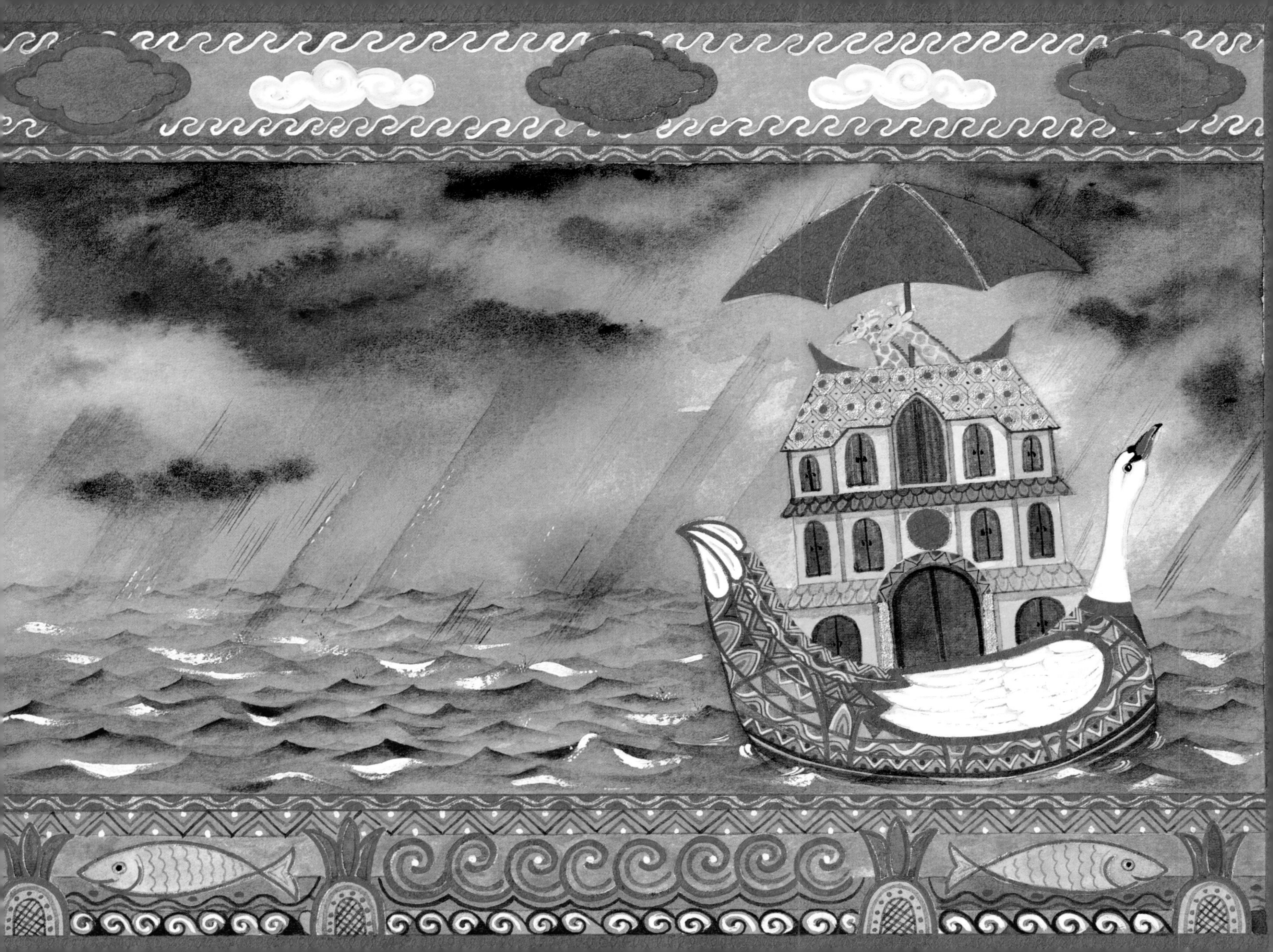

But all that time the Devil-mouse was nibbling away at one of the planks of Noah's ark, trying to make a hole so that the ark would fill with water, sink, and drown them all.

At last the Devil chewed all the way through the plank, and water began to gush into the ark.

When Noah heard the sound of water running, he knew that something bad had happened. He had made the ark carefully, just as God had told him to, and it should not have sprung a leak.

He went to look, and saw the mouse, gnawing at the hole. "You devil!" he said, and he threw his fur glove at it.

As the glove whirled through the air, it turned into a cat. The cat pounced and, in the twinkling of an eye, caught the mouse in her mouth.

Now, in all the weeks on the water Noah had never allowed any fighting on the ark, and he would not start now. So he picked up the cat and threw her overboard, with the mouse in her mouth.

When the cat fell into the cold water, she opened her mouth wide with the shock, and so the Devil escaped to play his wicked tricks another day.

The cat swam back to the ark, and climbed aboard, and then she found the sunniest spot of all and lay down to get warm and dry. And that is why to this day cats hate to get wet, and like to curl up in a sunny spot and bask in the sun.

So the cat was all right, but the water was still pouring through the hole that the mouse had made, and if Noah could not stop it, they would all drown.

No one could think of what to do, except the wily snake, who said, "If I plug the hole, what will you give me?"

"What do you want?" asked Noah.

"After the flood, I want you to give me a human being every day, for me and my children to eat."

And Noah had no choice but to say, "Yes."

With that, the snake cut off its own tail, and stuffed it into the hole so that the water could not come in. And that is why, ever since, snakes have no tails.

For a hundred and fifty days the ark floated on the water, and then God allowed the flood to subside, and the ark came to rest on the highest peak of Mount Ararat.

Noah opened a window in the ark, and set free a dove, to fly and search for dry land. For seven days she circled the ark, but she could find nowhere to land, so Noah reached out his hand and took her back into the ark.

A week later Noah set the dove free once more. This time she flew away, and in the evening when she returned, she had a sprig of fresh olive in her beak. It was the first growing thing that Noah had seen since the beginning of the flood. After seven more days he set the dove free again, and this time she did not return.

At last the land was dry.

So Noah and his sons, Shem, and Ham, and Japheth, opened the great door in the ark and let it down so that it made a gangplank. Two by two, the animals and birds left the ark and trotted and flew to freedom, until at last the only creatures left on board were the cat, who was curled up, purring in the sun, and Noah's wife, who didn't want to leave the ark, which had been such a happy home for so long.

"Come out," said Noah.

"No," said his wife.

"Come out," begged Noah.

"No," said his wife.

She really was a stubborn woman.

"Please," said Noah.

"Oh, all right," said his wife, and she walked down the gangplank, and the cat came with her.

Then Noah and his family knelt down and thanked God for saving them from the great flood. And when God saw them kneeling there, and the animals running free, and the birds singing for joy as they wheeled and swooped through the air, he said in his heart that he would never again try to destroy his creation. "While this world endures," he said, "the round of seedtime and harvest, heat and cold, summer and winter, day and night, shall never end."

God told Noah and his family, and all the animals and birds, "Be fruitful, and multiply, and replenish the earth." And he said to Noah, "These animals and birds I put into your care. Look after them, and remember that no man should kill another man."

Then God created the rainbow and set it as a shimmering beauty in the sky. "This is my sign to you," God said, "that I will never again destroy this wonderful world which I have made."

And Noah and his family rejoiced. Noah lit a fire, to make a thanksgiving sacrifice to God.

At that moment the snake slithered up, and said, "I kept my side of the bargain. Will you keep yours?"

Noah remembered his promise that every day he would give the snake a human being to eat. And he said to himself, "There are so few of us left. God has told us to replenish the earth and to look after the animals and birds. But if I give the snake a person to eat every day, soon we will all be gone."

So Noah seized the snake and threw it into the fire, where it was burned to ash. Then God sent a wind to scatter the ash all over the world, and from each fleck of ash a flea was born.

Noah lived until he was nine hundred and fifty years old, perfectly happy but for one small thing. For the rest of his days he and his wife, and Shem, and Ham, and Japheth and their wives, and their children, and their children's children, were plagued by fleabites.

And from that time to this, in fulfillment of Noah's promise to the snake, together all the fleas in the world suck just enough blood from people to make up one whole human being a day.

A NOTE ON THE STORY

I have woven this story from a handful of legends about Noah and his ark, the originals of which can be found in Moses Gaster's *Rumanian Bird and Beast Stories* (London: Published for the Folk-Lore Society by Sidgwick & Jackson, Ltd., 1915). This is a rich gathering of pourquoi tales, full of fascinating stories about how the animals were created, and why they behave as they do.

Moses Gaster (1856–1934) came to England in 1885, exiled from Romania for his part in helping Sephardic Jews settle in Palestine. He became the chief rabbi of the Sephardic community in England, and also a prominent folklorist whose scholarship still stands up today. He collected the tales from a variety of printed sources, and remembered hearing some of them himself as a child. They were, he wrote, "believed in implicitly" by the Romanian peasants who had preserved them in their oral tradition.

Like most folktales, the Romanian stories about Noah are not exclusive to one country. Similar tales were told across Eastern Europe; a Russian version, for instance, can be found in W. R. S. Ralston's *Russian Folk-Tales* (London: Smith, Elder, & Co., 1873). In Aarne and Thompson's *The Types of the Folktale* (Helsinki: Academia Scientiarum Fennica, 1961), the story of "The Devil in Noah's Ark" is assigned the international tale-type number AT825. Francis Lee Utley's essay "Noah, His Wife, and the Devil" (in Raphael Patai, ed., *Studies in Biblical and Jewish Folklore*, Bloomington: Indiana University Press, 1960) is an exhaustive study based on 280 variants of the tale.

But of all the versions, the Romanian tales seem to me the liveliest and freshest—full of sly humor and spot-on observation. Another of Gaster's stories, "Why Do Cats Eat Mice?," sets a similar tale in the time of Adam and Eve. This time it is Adam who builds a boat, hoping to sail away across the sea to somewhere the Devil cannot follow; but the Devil coils round Eve's bosom in the shape of a snake and so comes on board. As in the Noah story, the Devil then takes the form of a mouse and gnaws away at the planking. When Adam sees what is going on, he throws his fur glove, which changes into a cat, which eats up the Devil. This explains why a cat's fur will give off sparks, and why a cat's eyes glisten in the dark, for there are sparks of the Devil in every cat.

The Devil has a special place in Romanian folk belief. In his childhood memoir, quoted in Mabel Nandriş's *Folk Tales from Roumania* (London: Routledge and Kegan Paul, 1952), the folklorist Ion Creangă (Ion Stefanescu) describes "throwing stones into the bed of the river—one for God and one for the Devil, turn about, giving each his fair share." In a fascinating essay, "The Devil in Roumanian Folklore" (in *Folk-Lore*, vol. XL, 1929), Agnes and Helen B. Murgoçi show how to the Romanian peasant "the Devil is a very real person." They quote many Romanian proverbs, such as "Bow down before God, but don't quarrel with the Devil," which preserve a rough-and-ready folk wisdom rather similar to Noah's robust practicality.

The myth of the great flood appears in many of the world's cultures, and the story of Noah and the ark has been an inspiration for the folklore of Jews and Muslims as well as Christians. The Jewish legends—conveniently gathered in volume one of Louis Ginzberg's *The Legends of the Jews* (Philadelphia: The Jewish Publication Society of America, 1909)—tell how even Noah had so little faith that "he did not enter the ark until the waters had risen to his knees." Meanwhile, a Muslim commentator recounts how as the animals entered the ark, Noah touched and counted them. The ass was slow in boarding, and Noah called out, "Hurry, even though Satan be with thee," thus giving the Devil his chance.

The very idea of the ark and the animals catches the imagination. Even today, expeditions regularly search Mount Ararat, hoping to discover Noah's ark—their findings are surveyed in Lloyd R. Bailey's *Noah: The Person and the Story in History and Tradition* (Columbia: University of South Carolina Press, 1989). More exciting to me, Wildscreen Trust, the educational charity based in Bristol, England, is now establishing a "virtual ark." Their Arkive project will be a massive computerized database of all the world's endangered species—even the insects. Which do not, I guess, include the fleas . . .

Neil Philip